"Gary Whited has written a collection of poems about rural, western landscapes. His poetry brings readers along fence posts where western characters prevail: rattlesnakes, magpies, hawks and horses. His characters are startled by the earth as the poet is, and brings us there to the simplicity of earthly matters. Whited's poetry reminds me to observe the slow movement of time."

—Kristen Lodge, author of *Continental Quotient*

"Gary Whited's poems are a moving evocation of a truly iconic American landscape and culture, and a past we all share, that mysterious and sometimes frightening passage we call childhood. It has been a great privilege to witness the evolution of this work which has a deceptive simplicity but whose emotional depths inspire repeated reading."

—Dorothy Derifield, member of Jamaica Pond Poets,
and Director of Chapter and Verse Literary Series

"What gives this love-song to the prairies of Eastern Montana its heft and depth is not only the poet's deep affection for 'rattlesnake skins fluttering in the wind' and 'the perfection of still water' just below the muzzle of his father's white horse, but the way this love occurs amidst the disturbing sorrows and unspoken loneliness of these families in their struggles with themselves as well as the land. *Having Listened*, indeed, to the all of it, every wrinkle and sparrow, as well as his own darker side steeping like black tea in the cup of the self. And then the ancient voice out of the deep past, Parmenides, steadying him as he makes his way in the ubiquitous wind, like the 'badger, who digs alone into the sod and the silence.'"

—Roger Dunsmore, author of *You're Just Dirt*

"A gentle deferral lies at the center of Gary Whited's *Having Listened*. It's not about what he thinks or declares, but about the fruits of patient listening. Fathers and fence posts, horses, prairie and creek beds, speak in subtle flow, silence, poise or uneasiness. Deference to the sharp or subtle splendor of the place frame the poems collected here—verse occasionally broken by a wise remark from Parmenides or an occasional prose reverie. The surprise and afterglow is memorable. I've returned often to the tunings offered here: astonishing, wonderful, drifting by like prairie wind.

—Ed Mooney is author of *Lost Intimacy in Western Thought*,
and *Postcards Dropped in Flight*

"Each one of Gary Whited's poems is as fixed in place and time as a fence post on a snow-swept prairie in Montana, 'holding the barbed wire under / the wounding staples'; each poem a listening post that's staked at the crossroads of language and silence. These are serious and beautiful meditations on nature and family and hard work, detached yet possessed, as vigilant to elemental existence as they are entranced by it. Everywhere the writing is fully alive to the world it has so feelingly made."
   —George Kalogeris, author of *Dialogos, Paired Poems in Translation*

"For those of us who have known for many years the pleasures of Gary Whited's quiet, prairie-steeped poems, it is cause for celebration to finally see his work collected and in print. We have waited a long time for this haunting, elegiac book."
   —Aimée Sands, author of *The Green-go Turn of Telling*

HAVING LISTENED

HAVING
LISTENED

Gary Whited

POEMS

HOMEBOUND
PUBLICATIONS
Independent Publisher of Contemplative Titles
STONINGTON, CONNECTICUT

For bulk ordering information or permissions write:
Homebound Publications, PO Box 1442
Pawcatuck, Connecticut 06379 United States of America
Visit us at: www.homeboundpublications.com

FIRST EDITION
ISBN: 978-1-938846-19-9 (pbk)

Throughout the text, there are passages taken from
fragments of the poem by the ancient Greek, Parmenides.
The translation from the Greek is the author's.

BOOK DESIGN
Front Cover Image: © Sascha Burkard (shutterstock.com)
Cover and Interior Design: Leslie M. Browning

Library of Congress Cataloging-in-Publication Data

Whited, Gary.
  Having Listened / by Gary Whited. —first edition.
     pages cm
  "Throughout the text, there are phrase[s] and passage[s] taken from the poem of the ancient Greek, Parmenides. The translation from the Greek is the author's"—T.p. verso.
  ISBN 978-1-938846-19-9 (Paperback)
  1. Prairies—Fiction. I. Title.
  PS3623.H57975H38 2013
  813'.6--dc23
                                                          2013023646

10 9 8 7 6 5 4 3 2 1

Homebound Publications holds a fervor for environmental conservation. Our books are printed on paper with chain of custody certification from the Forest Stewardship Council, Sustainable Forestry Initiative, and the Programme for the Endorsement of Forest Certification. This ensures that, in every step of the process, from the tree to the reader's hands, the paper our books are printed on has come from sustainably managed forests.

Acknowledgments

My thanks to the editors of the following publications in which the following poems first appeared, some in slightly different versions:

Atlanta Review,	Startled by Earth (titled, Before the First Word)
The Aurorean,	This Urge for Here
Bellowing Ark,	Yellow in My Kitchen
	My Blue Shirt
Plainsongs,	Farm (titled, Remembering the Farm)
Red Owl Magazine,	Note to Parmenides (titled, For a Moment)
Salamander,	Ever
Comstock Review,	Taking Account

for Elizabeth

Contents

On this way are very many signs, that being is birthless
  and indestructible, for it is whole limbed and unmoved
    and without end; not ever was it or will it be, since it is now,
      all at once, one, continuous.

                    Parmenides
                    5th Century BCE
                    —FROM FRAGMENT VIII

*Come then, I will tell you, and you having heard the speech
give heed to it and carry it safely home.*

Parmenides
—FROM FRAGMENT II

Prairie

Wind sweeps across this picture

Meadowlark on barbed wire, yellow breasted door
    opens with its song

Weathered fenceposts hold the wire

Below the ground they slowly rot

Wind almost everyplace in this picture

Shirts on the clothes line, their sleeves ripple

The rattlesnake suns her long body on the scoria outcropping,
    her skin flutters above her like worn flags

Magpie flickers through chokecherry bushes
    at the edge of the creek

The black fruit sweetens in the long light

Beneath the wind

Do not forget the badger, who digs alone
    into the sod and the silence

While high above, wind carries the Rough-legged hawk
    on her long hunt

Over wheat fields that move in waves across the field,
    each stalk tossing its head like water

And as far as eye can see,
    the shadow of anything standing ripens twice each day

To Fencepost

It knew my breath
and knew my cheek.
It was yesterday,

a long time ago,
when I stood alone
next to any old fencepost

and waited before I knew
I was beginning
a practice of listening to what stands still

a long time.
Today, standing anyplace,
that yearning might come

for a way in
to where fenceposts stay without ceasing,
each one a priest of stillness.

Any day this is so—
on a hillside where wind trembles the grass
stands a quiet gray weathered post,

crust of golden lichen
glowing
on the shadowed side.

Shadwell Creek

...by the barn, chokecherry bushes
bristling thick along the bank,
to the east the bridge that thundered

underneath when horses passed;
small pools of mud after rain
damp and smelling of decay;

in the cool air, murmur of pigeons
among the bridge's girders
broken by the sudden rush of wing beats...

west, down the creek, the twig-crack
of deer leaping free of thickets;
on the north bank a barbed wire fence

rusting from winter to winter,
a fierce hold on what cannot be seen;
south, the long slope up to open hills

where cows graze
in the great slow curve of time...

Night Hawk's Path

It happened the first time
on the dirt cow path
when I walked

behind the milk cow,
evening chore-time light
gliding across Shadwell creek

now shadowed for the night.
When I stood still,
that hum

no one ever talked about, coming
from the earth, moved
up my legs

into my hips, turning
this body into sound.
Light flared yellow,

gathered around haystacks,
fenceposts,
the cow and me.

Shadow Builders

Cedar, ash, elm or pine,
no matter the wood,
every fencepost sends out its shadow

that reaches far
as first light slips
over the edge of morning.

Each shadow
shortens
all morning long

until it vanishes
into the small dent of noon
and the builders of shadows pause.

The first moment noon tilts west
the work begins again,
and the dark tower stretches

out the other way,
for the king cannot make up his mind.
Then night and rest

unless the moon.

Thunderstorm

Before we heard it or saw it coming
came the rhythm of pounding hooves

horses at full gallop
one end of the pasture to the other

gather at the corner
toss their heads

turn
and race back.

Then the heavy thunder
barreled down over Shadwell creek

rumbling and reckless

breaking the steady pace of pitchforks
that bent our backs

our listening lifted up
into the thick darkness

bodies, straight as fenceposts,
tuned to the ground's trembling.

Grief in Fenceposts

I felt its reach riding horseback
in summer pastures, passing by
the proud posts always standing

at the spot where they were set,
holding the barbed wire under
the wounding staples.

Each post, once a tree that stood
along some creek, knows every sunrise
to sunset, each moon's wax and wane,

every season, every storm, the cow,
the deer, the meadowlark and hawk,
rattlesnake, magpie, badger and horse.

The grief in fenceposts, I felt it
pass into my own upright body,
learned trust at the side of each post,

and what I desire now, to stand, naked,
seeing everything from where I am,
faithful to the place.

Horses Could Take You There

If I could remember it and the names of the horses—
But I don't until stuck in traffic on the Jamaicaway

And the Red-tail lands on a nearby limb
The horses' names start to come back

Goldie, Red, Lightning, Lucky, Blue, Babe and Spike
The young Sharp-shinned I killed at the creek back then

Shooting BB's, again and again, the young hawk perfectly still
Sound of my mother's accordion the only thing that soothed

If I'd ever believed in a god, this would be the time to unfold it
Travel to the other world was possible according to Parmenides

Horses could take you there
So quiet, the way Spike loped across the summer pasture

She devised Eros as the very first of all the gods...

Parmenides
— FROM FRAGMENT XIII

Startled by Earth

Fresh lit
on an early morning,
a candle flame

offers a voice
so clear, so yellow,
so inviting that I listen.

There, before silence
leans into sound,
I hear the cow birthing her calf;

her groans and heaves,
the slip and slide of it,
her long curving licks

cleaning the new body of light
startled by earth;
her rough-hewn tongue

giving voice to urges
so deep my own pelvic bowl
stirs for words

that have not yet fallen
from the tongue I carry
for a morning like this,

before the first word.

Ever

As if the old granary smell
    would ever vanish,

or the cedar fenceposts
    never rot off.

As if the harnesses hanging in the hayloft
    would ever shed all those spider webs,

maybe someday even, find the sweaty back
    and haunch of another horse.

As if the dealer at the Ranger Bar would ever smile,
    the bartender show above her knees,

or my father drive the old truck home
    in time for evening's barn chores.

As if any of us would stay there waiting
    beside the one gray and open door.

Yellow in My Kitchen

To the eye just coming out from winter,
the teapot hums its Norwegian yellow.

Beside it, the lemon, tipping like planet earth
with its equator arranged for summer,

sets my mouth to watering
the way it always does when I walk past

old yellow VW bugs that I want to bite
for that juicy sweet tart confabulation

my mouth creates from some half
remembered day in second grade

when we tasted something yellow.

On the table twelve roses stand erect
in their rectangle vase, drinking clear water

to feed their flaxen curving petals
that I long to be folded into the way

the blonde and abundant stack of oat hay
wrapped around me

when I leapt from the barn roof
to tumble for one moment of abandon

to be buried, to be touched
on every part of me by the full embrace

that oats always promised.

Thirst

The water bag
made of sewn canvas
with a lid at the mouth

the size of a silver dollar
hung from its rope handle
in the shadow

beneath the tractor seat,
while around the seams
swirling field-dust joined with seepage,

a soft and delicate film of mud,
spreading like lace across the canvas
that kept the water fresh,

and in the stillness of nothing
moving but a hawk circling above
and a whirling dance of dust,

he gathered up the damp rounded
sac, unloosed its clasp
and brought its mouth to his lips.

Eden

blue wind shaped the first guitar,
made it ocean, made it swimming tigers,
made it shine light to that face only my
hands could find, made it yellow the edges
of old albums, made it cosmos,
made it chicken house, windmill
and water tank holding, made me long
for the sea, dive deep, my eyes
find bright coral glowing, made grass
blow under the east wind, brought
sound spilling from every tongue over lips
full-kissed when god touched the tree, touched me,
touched you, carved words, touched our hips
to dance, spun our blood into new marrow,
called it love, called it mud, hawk, turtle,
called it here, called you mine, called me yours,
called everything until calling stuttered our lips
to silence, to kiss, to lie still, to hold tight,
to let this go

... according to belief, these things were brought forth and now are, and afterwards, from this time, they will grow and perish.

Parmenides
—FROM FRAGMENT XIX

My Father's Trips to Town

What a shy gentleman he was,
in the field, working,
in the church, silent,
unwilling to sing,

and in the bank,
head bowed, bargaining
with only the promise
of harvest.

Yet, in the bar, loosened
by liquor, laughing,
dice-shaking,
dare-taking beyond his reach;

at last, returning home after dark,
he walked alone, scolded,
to the barn
to milk the burdened cow

who lashed him in his shame
with her piss-wet tail
as he sat, cursing,
on the three-legged milking stool.

His Religion

Thundered sky, tattered by lightning,
comes back whole but blackened,
clouds full with the promise of rain.

My father looks west from the barn
before descending the rickety wooden steps
to the corral and his one Holstein cow

waiting just beyond sunup for oats
by the door where she always waits
and to be relieved of the load brimming in her udder,

the fresh milk she's been making all night
while these clouds gathered,
filling with what by late afternoon

could be hail instead of rain, his biggest worry,
what makes him light another cigarette,
wondering if his fields will be saved

from the hail stones' torture,
his wheat crop gone in minutes.
His hands protect the match's wobbly flame,

his deep breath sets the cigarette on fire,
its smoke rising, his ritual, his prayer.

My Mother's Accordion

When she opened its velvet-lined case,
its black and white ivory body
shone, as I believed the Holy Ghost

was supposed to. She had to let it take
the warmth by the stove before moving
its accordioned body. While we waited

her face began to shine. Maybe the Holy
Spirit was doing its work, lifting
the load of her worried world

off the small shoulders
I was using. When it was time,
she lifted it onto her body,

hooked the velvet straps
over her shoulders and unsnapped
its pleated bellows that opened wide

to let in the silent air. As she began
to work it in and out, sounds rose
from inside its ivoried box

that turned into old Norwegian tunes
I'd heard her hum, and her face
took a turn toward a song

she wanted the world to be.

Goldie and Red

In the full of winter my father would come past the house with the team and the hayrack on its large wooden sled runners, covered with iron so to wear longer, and I'd climb up with him, bundled in my layers of wool and overshoes, feeling thick within my own body, and we'd drive Goldie and Red to the field where the loaf-shaped haystacks had waited since July or August, to pitch the hay, fork-full at a time into the rack, to bring it home to the cows behind the barn in that pasture we fondly called "the milk-cow pasture."

I'd watch his pitchfork work in dimensions beyond me, large fork-fulls of hay rising as if some engine were lifting them, arcing from haystack to wagon rack, arriving in round bunches, heavy and silent, my own small three-tined fork offering only symbols of hay next to his volumes. We'd switch part way, front to back, so both ends of the rack would fill evenly, and my smallness would be swallowed in the heft of his work.

Then homeward, precarious on the pile of hay, holding the reins in my mittened hands while he gets off to open gates, and I drive through alone and mighty atop this masterpiece of work, which I fancy is mine for a moment as we pass out of sight of him closing the gate, until I try to stop the horses whose bitted mouths do not feel my tugs, and they move as if I am not there, when suddenly his voice booms from behind, "Whoa you sons-a-bitches, whoa!" and they stop as the reins go slack in my hands.

From The Well

In winter trouble rode the wind and snow to touch
her face with its stiff hand.

In summer my father dug a well with our white horse
walking circles way into the night.

Neighbors who gathered to help saw my mother's
eyes travel far away.

Hiding inside the attic, I read that Marco Polo returned
from far away with jewels sewn inside his coat.

Walking to the well, I took comfort in these words
and the water's burbling

clear and cool from the well. When evening came,
the red-haired cows made their dusty way

to water. The thirsty black-tailed deer waited
for the dark of night.

While the windmill turned, I waited to hear my name
one more time from my father's tongue.

If love has not been kind to my mother,
what can love do now?

Farm

My mother stood at her kitchen window
facing north and wringing her hands

Heavy like iron that I thought
I could unwind her gnarl of worry

When my father fixed fence along the creek
he expected supper   She unwound

her worried hands to make it
A mix of potatoes   meat   and sorrow

My father ate everything
except the sorrow—

My brother and I divided it
He   being older

took the smaller share
Evening came

I walked to the barn
to gather the cows

to smell the water in the cattle tank
to imagine I was a fin

on the windmill
a splinter on the fencepost

holding the gate

Elegy

for F.E.W.

Each January, this one day sweeps
my chest. I picture his white horse

stand motionless beside him,
my mother trudge snow up that hill,

kneel, hear his final rattle
and feel forsaken by her god,

as she has told it to me.
I've worked this day of the year,

telling it again and again, as if spoken words
could rub it smooth, as ocean waves

wear great stones round and soft to touch,
and still I feel its rough edge.

Story in One Sentence

... prairie for a visit this summer, as usual, only this time I didn't go alone because my kids, my daughter and my son, wanted to see their grandmother, who they hadn't seen for several years, been failing lately, down to 98 pounds from a husky Norwegian homesteader's daughter and has been losing it upstairs too, all of which sparked my kids into wanting to see her, knowing it could be the last time they saw her when she could still see them, which she's been wanting for a while now, knowing too that the end is in sight and wanting everything to be okay, even though it never has been from her perspective and won't be unless my kids are baptized Lutheran and accept Jesus as their savior, requiring that they first accept needing to be saved, which no way in hell will happen given the way I've raised them, making a big sore spot between my mother and me, nothing new really, though now I have to admit I'd like to ease my mother's soul along its way despite the fact I left the Lutheran fold long ago and can't bring myself to tell her I believe I'm a sinner and in need of saving anymore than my kids think this about anybody, while in spite of all this, she goes on "hoping things will be alright," which I've learned means she actually has no faith at all that they will be and goes on worrying about our souls all the time even when I assure her that we're spiritually really okay, knowing nothing I say soothes her for more than a moment, but I will say that at the end of our visit when saying our goodbyes she seemed to lift up out of her worry-world as my kids laughed and joked with her, crinkling her face into smiles and laughs like I hadn't seen maybe ever, when upon hearing my son tell her he loved her, she smiled half way across the prairie, and at that very moment I swear I saw the Holy Ghost enter the room and a little flame dance on top of her head.

... all is full at once of light and hidden night...

Parmenides
—FROM FRAGMENT IX

Betrayal

The horses are different
but the saddles are the same.

To those of us who follow the rules
we learned, falling in love

falls out of bounds. Getting bucked off,
every time, we have to land.

Homesteaders, bless them, filled the prairie
with a darkness they brought

from the old country. It did not vanish
in the big sky, nor in the little

white church where my mother
worshipped, where they taught us

to believe in the old religion, then
took love, or its echo, away.

If I'm not saddled with those beliefs,
please God, don't ignore my doubts.

The ones who betrayed me must have known,
someday I'd remember,

even if they were gone.

Manure

Its muted odor
   caught in the maw

of December's freeze
   as we slept in the flimsy shack

beside the coal furnace's
   smolder singing

into the wind's whistle
   around the loose window;

its rich smell
   in spring thaw,

its heft
   woven into winter's straw

where the heifers
   slept at night

bunched together
   against the rush of wind;

and the words waiting
    beneath my tongue

to melt into voice
    what was frozen

in the silence
    kept by everyone

who spoke,
    and the long wait…

After a Blizzard

In this arc of snow
    now hanging over the creek bank

in the windless air,
a stillness so silent and at rest
    I could not hold it,

for there was my faithless looking

to find a blemish in the clean edge,
or the hint of a dark secret
    under the curved lip of perfection.

When it wasn't to be found,
    I couldn't help the mitten touch

to disturb the virgin snow,
bring it too into the fallen place
    I knew,

while what I longed for
was just to breathe, kneel down
    and never move again.

Bunkhouse

The bunkhouse held a secret it carried for years.
Just walking near I'd feel an arm reaching out,

wanting something. I'd hold my breath
to keep it still, then walk fast to the creek

to hide, again, the freckled arm of the hired man.
When others walked nearby,

I'd wonder how they missed it.
We moved and it collapsed.

I didn't need a creek to hide things.
I walked like others,

as if no arm ever reached for me.
It worked for a long time

until the day I heard they burned down
what was left of the bunkhouse.

Everywhere I walked, I startled to see arms
coming out of walls.

Beside the Barn

A monstrous want to know
rooted in deaf dirt

where buried all

that happened out of sight,

still
it happened.

Come close enough
to touch this fragile web

a carried story

frayed from travel
into voice

where anyone can hear
who listens,

but no one touches.

In this Body

There are rooms
that close their doors.
Years pass

and a breeze moves through.
Maybe it was the look of that man
with red hair and heavy hands,

or the woman crossing the street
with the soft fingers
and far away stare.

A door blows open slightly,
the hinges barely agree.
Behind that door

there's a small child
who wants you
to call him by name.

Here I end my trustworthy account and thought concerning truth;
from here on learn the opinions of mortals…

Parmenides
—from Fragment VIII

Beginning with a Click on the Handle

We all knew the ceiling of the tipped shack
that old homesteader made his home for sixty
years wanted to cave in, but nobody knew
the wisdom of his mattress where his money molded

while his horse dozed, one hind foot cocked
against the frozen manure, to rest under
the still-steaming harness,
his hired man smoking and fondling

the slack reins, and me there burying secrets beneath
the heavy lids where Lutherans kept everything,
their handles all broken, and I, bearing that weight
as if it were my gravity—

Ink and Sin

This morning I sit down with my new fountain pen, fill it carefully from the reservoir at the side of the bottle, slowly replace the lid and screw it tight. Then I begin to write across the empty page—so smooth this indelible black ink flows into words, and so smooth my memory slides back to when I was little, and Grandma wrote letters back home to Missoura, with fountain pens that filled from ink bottles I loved to touch, to watch the dark body of ink sway inside the smooth glass walls with the slightest wobble. Each tilt aroused the sly fear of a spill I knew would make an indelible mark across her desk, her paper, the carpet, someplace everyone would see; like sin, as I was taught by my mother and the Lutherans. Grandma wasn't a Lutheran, but she had a face that could fire up a fear just like the image of hell that floated through the church pews Sunday mornings.

I'd sit quiet in church watching my mother's face go stone-still, hard in the eyes, harder than the wooden pew that squeaked with a subtle yawn, or a slow turn of the head straining to see what the men were doing on the benches at the back, crows gone to sleep along a limb where no wind blew, heads tilting at angles of repose, shirt pockets bulging with packs of cigarettes I knew they'd light up as soon as they walked outside at the end of all the talk from the pulpit about fire and sin and the savior's hands receiving the awful nails for us, always for us.

At my Grandma's desk I'd weigh the odds, take a careful twist to test how tight the lid was closed, then tilt the bottle slightly to watch the black body of ink climb one side then the other, leaving, for moments, a thin veil of itself clinging to the inside walls of the darkened glass. Wasn't it trying to leave this glassy prison, waiting to be drawn into the small barrel of the green or the red pen, waiting to become a letter of the alphabet, a word in one of Grandma's sentences, then to dry and lie still across the crisp white paper from her thick tablet and be folded inside an envelope with a three cent stamp? She'd send me off to the post office, across the street at the end of her block, then across the other street to the red brick building with "U.S. POST OF-FICE" etched in the stone lintel over the door.

Once inside, another world shone off the murals of Freder-ick Remington, off the shiny marble floor, and off the walls where "WANTED" posters showed tough faces of people I knew had sinned, spilled blood maybe, like ink, across someone's shirt, and now their face was on the wall for all to see. I'd shiver at the thought that my face could appear there, hold my breath as I slid past the bulletin board and over to the mail slot, where I'd read three times to make sure it was the one Grandma had shown me, where letters were supposed to go. Finally I'd let it fall from my hand, wondering if I'd done it right. When I was sure I'd done nothing wrong, my mind would fly off into its wondering about that ink, now stilled onto Grandma's letter, with its job of saying something to someone far off in Missoura, who I'd never met, but knew was waiting to hear how we were doin'. I longed for a job so clear, so clean, so done now that no sin could happen by mistake by my hand, or mind, which still moved, like the ink in the bottle, and anything was waiting to happen in this world where a sin could put your face on one of those posters, forever.

Incantation

First crow call caught the morning
   bright as yellow Easter eggs.
      I awake to prayer—

Scavenge here on my sleep
   you black-winger,
      open it wide. Give me

your sliver of dark, whole.
   Let the pierce of your voice pick
      me skeleton-clean. Prey

with that black beak of yours
   in my small church
      mind where dark ones

sleep. Let my bones shatter
   into glyphs. Throw me
      your trust oh dark one,

peck through my buried holding back.

Winnowing

Wind against the weight of things,
    the chaff, the straw, the wheat
makes it all happen.
    You don't have to.

Song for Clothespins

Hold on, hold on,

the wire, the wire,

     don't ever ...

The wind
they need to dry
those sheets
     turned sails—

hold on,

     don't ever ...

The sun
that speeds the work of wind
turns gray
     the wooden pins

that hold

     that hold

End of Crying

Ornery walked up
cuffed Cringing on the head
walked off
saying something about
Dread

Worry stumbled
at the door
hat in hand
looked everyone in the eye
one more time

Wallowing-In-It
swaggered by
in his Cadillac
hit the brake
tossed a handkerchief
to Crying
and sped off
with Damn-It-All

A Lutheran Overcoming
the Doctrine of Original Sin

"No!" was what I heard,
tucked it into my shirt pocket—
the one on the left— and walked
into the rest of my life.

Worn with years, that pocket finally
frayed and opened, spilled all it held
onto the ground.

To my surprise, from a nearby tree
something clear spoke. I barely heard.
Its feathers brushed against my skin.

When my hands opened,
the world started over.
"Yes!" was almost its name.

Jazz on the Farm

after Mark Shilansky
jazz pianist

Walk like a cow to water
   teeter totter

water the horse the pig
   whistle whinny
   the white mare's skinny

skinny enough to whittle wind
   into the last dance
   last chance

to listen lovely tunes across
   into the night
   night the fox

can't catch the chicken
   big fat chicken
   we saved for the feast

the feast all them saints
   walk to with no water
   and sing this one last strum

last strum we hear nowhere
   no here
   now there at the corner

of her mouth
   we fall in love way too easy

Heist

Thin, like onion skin, the wax paper over the pastries
within reach on the bakery's shelf. Easy to imagine
lifting one small biscuit, dropping it into my grocery
bag, burdened already at the store next door by one
bottle of milk, two bunches of carrots, one sprig of Italian
parsley, six mushrooms and one garlic bulb. So easy, I lifted two
biscuits without a whisper of wax paper rattle and let them fall
beneath the carrot greens. An old man wearing orange
pants sat so close he had to see, but didn't flinch when I
walked past the lady, blouse untucked, hair dusted white
with flour, standing at the counter counting bills
and stacking quarters in pillars that tilted to one side.
Gravity might have tipped them over, but didn't,
and a strong urge came into my filching finger to nudge them.
Instead, I hurried to the door, stepped over the worn threshold
to the busted wooden step onto the brand new sidewalk.
Summer's heavy air gripped my wrists like handcuffs.
Stricken with fear of getting caught, I stepped deep
into a tall tree's shadow, swore to anyone who would listen—

"I didn't take the biscuits, the man didn't see, no untucked lady
stacked quarters. The threshold was new, the step was not
busted, and my bag has no carrots, milk, garlic or parsley.
Only the mushrooms are real."

The Kiss

This time don't leave the spoon in the soup pot
when it's still heating. You'll ruin it, you will,
and it's the one my aunt Charlotte gave to me

the day she kissed the mailman nobody liked.
Don't, please don't, think ill of me for saying it,
but I was so happy to hear that she'd kissed him

since nobody else ever had, I'm sure, and he walked
with greater torque in his stride from that day onward.
Mail never was late to our house after that, and she never

kissed him again either, for that night she fell ill with
that thing nobody ever found a name for, as many as
ten doctors tried and failed to nail it down, or give

her anything that ever brought relief. There was talk
in the house that she never should have kissed him,
but I don't think she would have had such a sweet

time being sick without that one and only kiss. Her
lips vibrated with it until the day she took that last
breath and the mailman stood outside the house

with his empty bag, having finished his route, waiting
for word–not if, but when–she passed, as he wanted
to know exactly the moment so he could leave the letter

he'd waited all that time to send, and could not find a carrier
worthy of delivering the simple little thing in its off-white
envelope, tiny face with lips drawn over the sealed edge.

So, as I said, never leave that spoon over the edge of the pot
when the fire's still burning. Aunt Charlotte would have
a conniption if she ever thought something happened to it.

It is one to me from what place I begin,
for to that place I come back again.

Parmenides
—from Fragment V

Having Listened

Trees were seldom, sunlight plentiful.
I roamed there among fenceposts that cut the light.
Each thin shadow spoke the day west to east,
trusted night, then reached again.
Any creature rising up offered its tongue of dark—
the hawk's quick fragment,
prairie dog's short poem,
buffalo an epic.

Note to Parmenides

One day the sun was shining
and I rode my father's white horse

across the wide summer pasture.
It must be that maidens of the sun guided me

for when I rode to the round wooden water tank
just before the mare's muzzle rippled the surface

I felt the perfection of still water
settle into my belly

and for a moment
nothing moved.

Then I listened as each swallow
passed down her long gullet.

When the water stilled again
we turned to leave.

Taking Account

On the roof pigeons, in the tree squirrels;
On the sidewalk hopscotch, in the back yard football;

On the seashore seaweed, on the prairie needle-grass;
In the book your name, over the altar candles;

On the outhouse a moon, on the chicken coop a rooster;
On the left I'm lonely, on the right I'm gone;

On the barbed wire a meadowlark, on the fencepost a hawk;
In the air your memory, in the pasture your horse;

In the envelope my whereabouts, on the stairway a thistle;
On the hour breaking news, in the moment this breath;

On the inside tender, on the outside weathered;
In the field a whirlwind, on the windmill a sparrow.

My Son's Philosophy Books

Sitting next to my son's books,
I feel their heft and the heat inside them.

So many words trying for exactly what we want to say.
If books were easy, we would never burn them.

My father's words were few,
but he had a thousand ways to curse the Russian thistles.

They grew big and round when nothing else would.
Dried and broken loose in Autumn,

they rolled with the wind against the nearest fence.
The thistles always won.

Some years we burned them, a fierce and fast fire.
My father ran from pile to pile,

a heap of flaming thistles on the end of his pitchfork.
I ran beside him, flames crackling in my ear.

Someplace among the burning
I felt he loved me.

Someplace beside these books
I feel the words catch fire, my son's eyes begin to glow.

If love was easy,
we'd forget how to burn thistles.

Philosopher

Words keep falling out of his chest,
    tumbling as birds from a nest
who find their wings, feather
    the tattered sky.

Someplace

Just as little is seen in pure light
as in pure darkness.
—HEGEL

Wind chimes next door
Listen, they sound free
Someplace a horse is running right now

Someplace a polar bear is resting on ice
Wind moves over the curve of earth like a glove
Listen, grass says, it is here

Any place opposites move toward the next imperfection
Wind, for example
Listen, you can hear leaves tremble

Someplace a grasshopper nibbles on the tender wheat
Stops to spit, chews, leaps to the next stalk
A child sees this, mimics it with his whole body

Listen, someplace we sing the last song
The place they pull us free from breathing this air

...it is not right that being be unlimited,
for it is not in need;
if it were it would need everything.

Parmenides
— FROM FRAGMENT VIII

Standing in Falling Snow

The even slant of it
    The sound
Near to nothing

On bare branches
    Stillness
Speaking to strangers

In Praise of Light

This morning a single horse chestnut rests beside me
on a white plate receiving a magnificent glow

over one shoulder of its well-rounded body. I watch it
and fall into imagining that it might be grateful

for the light that brought it here, for all the labor
of the dark tree near the library, grateful to the tree

to have arrived at some exact limb, to have gathered
the spiny shroud around it, to have pushed out

from its middle in all directions until the urge seized it,
with its exact weight, to let go, to take flight

for one moment of its entire life, to fall, to crack itself open.

My Blue Shirt

Hangs in the closet
of this small room, collar open,
sleeves empty, tail wrinkled.

Nothing fills the shirt but air
and my faint scent. It waits,
all seven buttons undone,

button holes slack,
the soft fabric with its square white pattern,
all of it waiting for a body.

It would take any body, though it knows,
in its shirt way of knowing, only mine,
has my shape in its wrinkles,

my bend in the elbows.
Outside this room birds hunt for food,
young leaves drink in morning sunlight,

people pass on their way to breakfast.
Yet here, in this closet,
the blue shirt needs nothing,

expects nothing, knows only its shirt knowledge,
that I am now learning—
how to be private and patient,

how to be unbuttoned,
how to carry the scent of what has worn me,
and to know myself by the wrinkles.

This Urge for Here

The sleeping dog by the stove,
the cardinal calling
in the maples out back,
that touch of wooden floor
on bare feet,
this taste of tea...

Oh urge, grow deeper,
help me stay here.

So still now,
only the black tea steeping
into its darker self.

Acknowledgments

I would first like to express my deep gratitude to all of the Jamaica Pond Poets; to everyone at the Brookline Poetry Series; and to the many folks at the William Joiner Center Writers' Workshop, for their listening and insightful reflections that have helped shape these poems. Special thanks to the guys of the international men's group, to many within the IFS community, and to Rich, Barbara and Ann for their faith and support; to Sarah, Bob, Helena, Chris and Paul for often being the first listeners; to Jamie for her coaching; to Ed, Roger and Sally, who encouraged from far away; and to Katherine and Tom, whose listening, love and friendship have been a steady presence all along the way.

I especially want to thank Fred Marchant for his inspired teaching, his friendship and his trust in this project over the long haul.

To the entire editorial staff at Homebound Publications, my deep appreciation for selecting *Having Listened,* and to Leslie Browning my heartfelt thanks for her guidance and generous help in bringing this book to completion.

I also want to thank Rhonda, Sherry, Ron and Sharon and all the rest back on the ranch for keeping it going.

And finally, thanks from the bottom of my heart and my ink well to Anna, Soren and Jeremy for indulging my writing habits and still trusting, and to Elizabeth who has been there listening forever and whose love along with her devotion to her work as a visual artist have inspired me always to keep going.

HOMEBOUND
PUBLICATIONS

AT HOMEBOUND PUBLICATIONS WE RECOGNIZE THE IMPOR-
TANCE of going home to gather from the stores of old wis-
dom to help nourish our lives in this modern era. We choose
to lend voice to those individuals who endeavor to trans-
late the old truths into new context and keep alive through
the written word ways of life that are now endangered. Our
titles introduce insights concerning mankind's present in-
ternal, social and ecological dilemmas.

It is our intention at Homebound Publications to re-
vive contemplative storytelling. We publish full-length in-
trospective works of: non-fiction, essay collections, epic
verse, short story collections, journals, travel writing, and
novels. In our fiction titles our intention is to introduce new
perspectives that will directly aid mankind in the trials we
face at present.

It is our belief that the stories humanity lives by give
both context and perspective to our lives. Some older sto-
ries, while well-known to the generations, no longer reso-
nate with the heart of the modern man nor do they address
the present situation we face individually and as a global vil-
lage. Homebound chooses titles that balance a reverence for
the old sensibilities; while at the same time presenting new
perspectives by which to live.

CPSIA information can be obtained
at www.ICGtesting.com
Printed in the USA
FFOW03n1110030614